This book belongs to

_____

To Kim and Sam

selected and illustrated by

MICHAEL HAGUE

LET'S READ!

TEDDY BEARS' MOTHER GOOSE

Henry Holt and Company · New York

CONTENTS

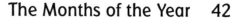

Teddy Bears' Mother Goose

Old Mother Goose, when
She wanted to wander,

Would ride through the air
On a very fine gander.

Mother Goose had a house,
'Twas built in a wood,
Where a bear at the door
For sentinel stood.

Rub-a-dub-dub,
Three bears in a tub,
And who do you think they be?
The butcher, the baker,
The candlestick-maker —
Turn 'em out, knaves all three.

Three wise bears of Gotham,
They went to sea in a bowl;
And if the bowl had been stronger,
My song might have been longer.

Bobby Shafto's gone to sea, silver buckles at his knee;
He'll come back and marry me, Bonny Bobby Shafto!

Bobby Shafto's fat and fair, combing down his yellow hair;
He's my love for evermore, Bonny Bobby Shafto!

Hector Protector was dressed all in green;
Hector Protector was sent to the Queen.
The Queen did not like him,
No more did the King;
So Hector Protector was sent back again.

Peter, Peter, pumpkin eater,
Had a wife and couldn't keep her;
He put her in a pumpkin shell,
And there he kept her very well.

There was an old bear who
lived in a shoe,
She had so many cubs
she didn't know what to do;

She gave them some honey
to spread on their bread,
Then kissed them all round
and sent them to bed.

There was a crooked bear,
And he went a crooked mile;
He found a crooked sixpence
Beside a crooked stile.
He bought a crooked cat,
Which caught a crooked mouse,
And they all lived together
In a little crooked house.

Little Tommy Tittlemouse
Lived in a little house;
He caught fishes
In other bears' ditches.

There was an old bear
Lived under a hill,
And if she's not gone
She lives there still.

There's a neat little clock,
In the schoolroom it stands,
And it points to the time
With its two little hands.
And may we, like the clock,
Keep a face clean and bright,
With hands ever ready
To do what is right.

Multiplication is vexation;
Division is as bad.
The Rule of Three
Doth puzzle me,
And Practice drives me mad.

Here am I,
Little Jumping Joan;
When nobody's with me
I'm all alone.

Here's Sulky Sue;
What shall we do?
Turn her face to the wall
Till she comes to.

Jack be nimble,
Jack be quick,
Jack jump over the candlestick.

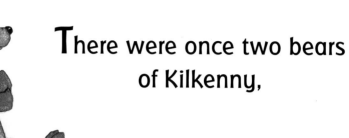

There were once two bears
of Kilkenny,

Each thought there was
one bear too many.

So they fought and they fit,
And they scratched and they bit,

Till, excepting their nails
And the tips of their tails,
Instead of two bears,
there weren't any.

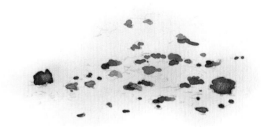

Great A, little a,
Bouncing B,
The cat's in the cupboard
And can't see me.

As I went to Bonner,
I met a pig
Without a wig,
Upon my word and honor.

This little teddy
went to market;
This little teddy
stayed home;
This little teddy
had roast beef;
This little teddy
had none;

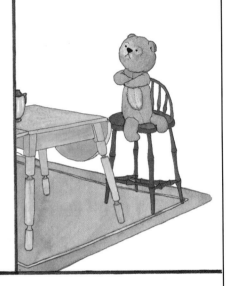

This little teddy said,
"Wee, wee! I can't find my way home."

Handy Pandy, Jack-a-dandy,
Loves plumcake and sugar candy;
He bought some at a grocer's shop
And out he came, hop, hop, hop.

The Bear in the Moon came tumbling down,
And asked the way to Norwich;
He went by the south, and burnt his mouth
With eating cold pease porridge.

Pease porridge hot,
Pease porridge cold,
Pease porridge in the pot,
Nine days old.
Some like it hot,
Some like it cold,
Some like it in the pot,
Nine days old.

Jack and Jill went up the hill
To fetch a pail of water;
Jack fell down and broke his crown,
And Jill came tumbling after.

Then up Jack got
and off did trot,
As fast as he could caper,
To old Dame Dob,
who patched his nob,
With vinegar and
brown paper.

Little Miss Muffet
Sat on a tuffet,
Eating her curds and whey;

There came a big spider,
Who sat down beside her,
And frightened Miss Muffet away.

To market, to market,
To buy a fat hog;
Home again, home again,
Jiggety jog.

To market, to market,
To buy a fat pig;
Home again, home again,
Jiggety jig.

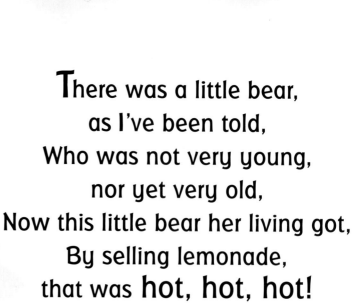

There was a little bear,
as I've been told,
Who was not very young,
nor yet very old,
Now this little bear her living got,
By selling lemonade,
that was hot, hot, hot!

Every teddy in this land
Has twenty nails,
upon each hand
Five, and twenty
on hands and feet.
All this is true,
without deceit.

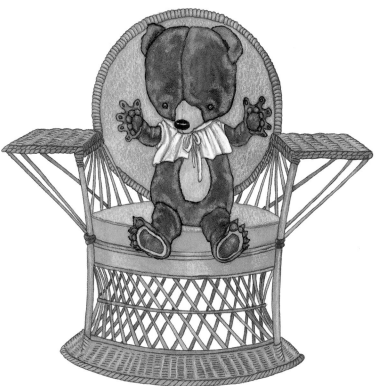

Little Jack Horner
Sat in the corner
Eating a Christmas pie;
He put in his thumb,
And pulled out a plum,
And said,
"What a good bear am I!"

Ride away, ride away,
Johnny shall ride,
And he shall have pussy-cat
tied to one side;
And he shall have little dog
tied to the other;
And Johnny shall ride
to see his grandmother.

Little Tom Tucker
Sings for his supper.
What shall we give him?
White bread and butter.
How shall he cut it
Without a knife?
How will he be married
Without a wife?

Polly, put the kettle on,
Polly, put the kettle on,
Polly, put the kettle on;
   And we'll have tea.

            Sukey, take it off again,
            Sukey, take it off again,
            Sukey, take it off again;
               They've all gone away.

Pat-a-cake, pat-a-cake, baker's bear,
Bake me a cake as fast as you dare;

Roll it, pat it, mark it with a T,
Put it in the oven for Teddy and me.

Jack Sprat could eat no fat,
His wife could eat no lean;
And so between them both, you see,
They licked the platter clean.

Cross patch, draw the latch,
Sit by the fire and spin;
Take a cup and drink it up,
Then call your neighbors in.

I love you well, my little brother,
And you are fond of me;
Let us be kind to one another,
As bear cubs ought to be.
You shall learn to share with me,
We'll play without any cares;
And then I think that we shall be
Two happy little bears.

Hark, hark!
The dogs do bark,
Beggars are coming to town:
Some in jags and some in rags
And some in velvet gown.

I like little Teddy,
His coat is so warm,
And if I don't hurt him,
He'll do me no harm;
So, I'll not pull his ears,
Nor run away,
But Teddy and I
Very gently will play.

Monday's bear is fair of face,

Tuesday's bear is full of grace,

Wednesday's bear is full of woe,

Thursday's bear has far to go,

Friday's bear is loving and giving,

Saturday's bear works hard for its living,

But the bear that is born on the Sabbath day
Is bonny and blithe, and good and gay.

January brings the snow,
Makes our feet and fingers glow.

February brings the rain,
Thaws the frozen lake again.

March brings breezes, loud and shrill,
To stir the dancing daffodil.

April brings the primrose sweet,
Scatters daisies at our feet.

May brings flocks of pretty lambs,
Skipping by their fleecy dams.

June brings tulips, lilies, roses,
Fills the children's hands with posies.

Hot July brings cooling showers,
Apricots, and gillyflowers.

August brings the sheaves of corn,
And the harvest home is borne.

Warm September brings the fruit;
Sportsmen then begin to shoot.

Fresh October brings the pheasant;
Then to gather nuts is pleasant.

Dull November brings the blast;
Now the leaves are whirling fast.

Chill December brings the sleet,
Blazing fire, and Christmas treat.

Christmas is coming, the geese are getting fat,
Please to put a penny in an old bear's hat;
If you haven't got a penny, a ha'penny will do;
If you haven't got a ha'penny, God bless you.

Cold and raw the north wind doth blow,
Bleak in the morning early;
All the hills are covered with snow,
And winter's now come fairly.

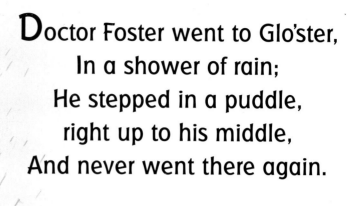

Doctor Foster went to Glo'ster,
In a shower of rain;
He stepped in a puddle,
right up to his middle,
And never went there again.

Rain, rain, go away,
Come again another day;
Little Teddy wants to play.

The bear in the wilderness
Asked me
How many strawberries
Grew in the sea.
I answered him,
As I thought good,
As many as red herrings
Grew in the wood.

Hush-a-bye, teddy,
on the treetop,
When the wind blows,
the cradle will rock;
When the bough breaks,
the cradle will fall,
Down will come teddy,
cradle and all.

Little Bear Blue,
Come, blow your horn,
The sheep's in the meadow,
The cow's in the corn;
But where is the little bear
Who looks after the sheep?
Under the haystack,
Fast asleep.

There was a little bear
went into a field,
And lay down
on some hay;

An owl came out
and flew about,
And the little bear
ran away.

Dickery, dickery, dare,
The pig flew in the air;
The bear in brown
soon brought him down,
Dickery, dickery, dare.

There was an old bear
tossed up in a basket,
Seventeen times
as high as the moon;
Where she was going
I couldn't but ask it,
For in her hand
she carried a broom.
"Old bear, old bear,
old bear," quoth I,
"Where are you going to
up so high?"
"To sweep the cobwebs
off the sky!"
"May I go with you?"
"Aye, by-and-by."

What is the news of the day,
Good neighbor, I pray?
They say the balloon
Is gone up to the moon!

Hey, diddle, diddle!
The cat and the fiddle,
The cow jumped over the moon;
The little bear laughed
To see such sport,
And the dish ran away with the spoon.

Diddle, diddle, dumpling,
my bear John,
went to bed
with his trousers on;
One shoe off,
and one shoe on,
diddle, diddle, dumpling,
my bear John.

Wee Willie Winkie
runs through the town,
Upstairs and downstairs
in his nightgown,
Rapping at the window,
crying through the lock,
"Are the teddies all in bed,
for now it's eight o'clock?"

The Bear in the Moon
looked out of the moon,
Looked out of the moon and said,
"'Tis time for all little bears on the earth
To think about getting to bed!"

Index of First Lines

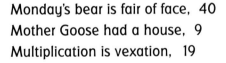

Henry Holt and Company, LLC
Publishers since 1866
115 West 18th Street
New York, New York 10011

Henry Holt is a registered trademark of Henry Holt and Company, LLC

Published in Canada by Fitzhenry & Whiteside Ltd.,
195 Allstate Parkway, Markham, Ontario L3R 4T8.
Library of Congress Cataloging-in-Publication Data
Teddy bears' Mother Goose / Michael Hague.
Summary: Mother Goose rhymes that feature teddy bears either in the text or the illustrations.
1. Nursery rhymes. 2. Children's poetry. 3. Teddy bears—Juvenile poetry.
[1. Nursery rhymes. 2. Teddy bears—Poetry.]
PZ8.3.H11935 Tes 2000 398.8—dc21 99-53629

ISBN 0-8050-3821-3
First Edition—2001
Printed in Hong Kong
1 3 5 7 9 10 8 6 4 2

The artist used pen and ink, watercolor, and pencil on watercolor board to create the illustrations for this book.